For Laria and her mother

L.B.

For Michel and Eliane

N.P.

MYRIAD BOOKS LIMITED
35 Bishopsthorpe Road, London SE26 4PA

First published in 2005 by
MIJADE PUBLICATIONS
16-18, rue de l'Ouvrage
5000 Namur-Belgium

© Laurence Bourguignon and Nancy Pierret, 2005

Translation: Lisa Pritchard

ISBN 1 84746 031 3

Printed in China

Laurence Bourguignon

THERE'S A MONSTER IN THE TOILET

Nancy Pierret

MYRIAD BOOKS LIMITED

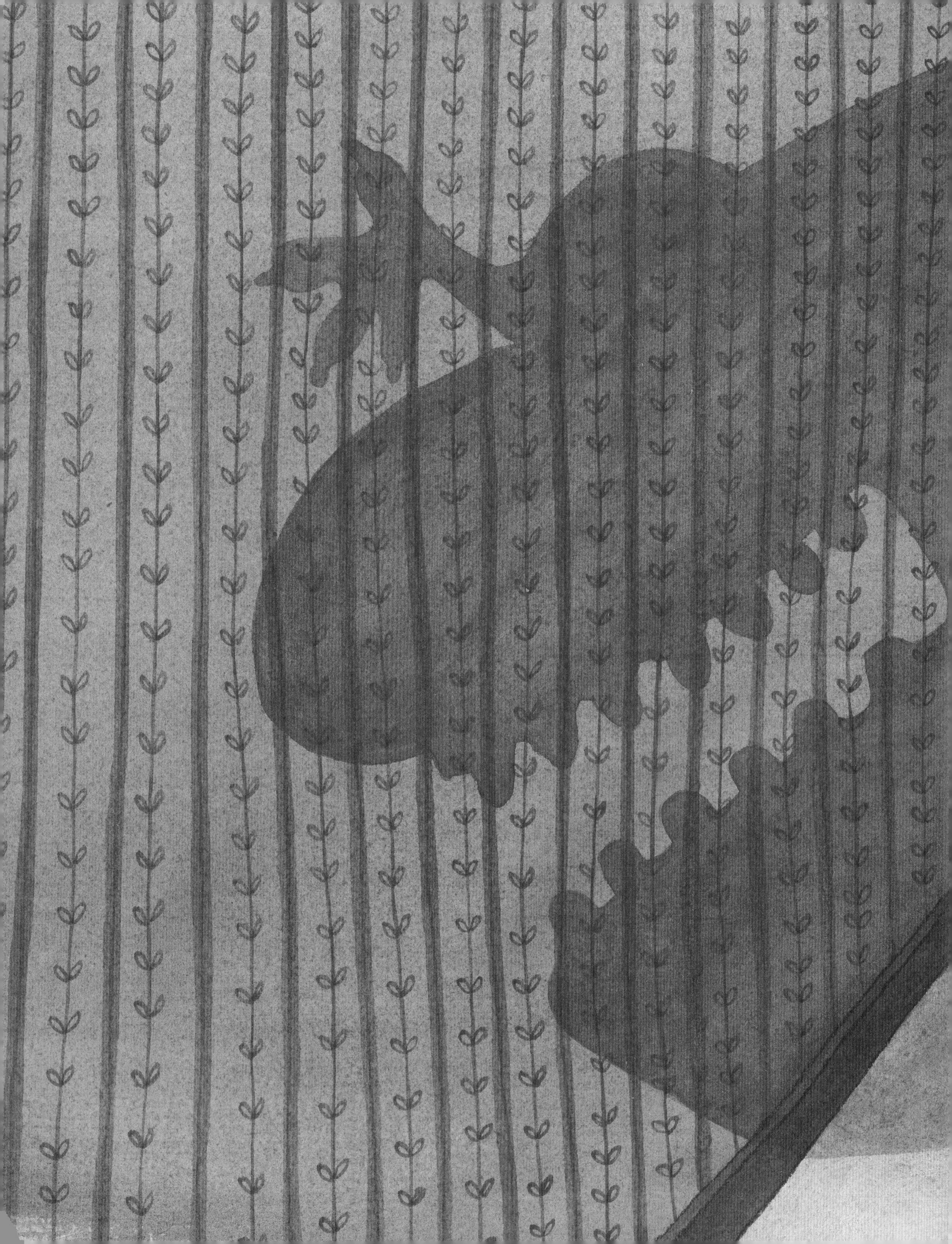

Max didn't like sitting on the toilet.

That big hole at the bottom of the toilet
bowl was scary. Where did it go?

BLOUB ! GLOUP !

Max didn't like flushing the toilet either. He would push the button and run out of the bathroom. He could hear the water gurgling and gargling. It sounded like a monster in the toilet.

Max wanted to use his potty, like he did when he was little.
But Mum said, "No, Max. You are a big boy now. Use the toilet."

That didn't make Max feel better. What if he fell down that big hole? How would he get out?
He made a long rope just in case…

But a rope wouldn't be much use if the monster decided to come out of its hole…

So Max made some special shoes for a quick getaway if the monster showed up.

Maybe it would be a good idea to stop the monster getting out. Max stuffed lots of toilet paper down the toilet.
Now there was no way out!

But later, when Max went back to check, he could hear Dad in the bathroom. He was very cross and the toilet was making strange noises.

When Dad came out he was all red in the face, and his arms were wet.
There was no sign of the monster anywhere.
Dad must have let it get away.

That evening Dad had a talk with Max. "You mustn't stuff lots of paper down the toilet. It stops the water going down the hole and makes it come out over the top of the toilet instead."

Max had to think of another way to deal with the monster.

What did the monster look like?
Max had no idea. But he was pretty
sure that it wasn't happy. After all,
it lived down the toilet. It never got
presents.
Max decided to give the monster a
present. Then it would be a happy
monster.

He threw a sweet in a bright green wrapper into
the toilet.
But the monster didn't come out to get it.
Perhaps it was scared of Max…

Every day Max sent the monster a little present down the toilet.
Now he really wanted to meet it – it was so shy.

Max put up lovely posters on the bathroom wall, so that if the
monster came out it would have a lovely surprise.

Maybe Max and the monster were the same age. Maybe it liked the same games. If it was a little boy monster, it would love the red car Max got for Christmas.

Max's car was super, with doors you could open and a shiny silver engine under the bonnet.
He tied it to a string and lowered it into the toilet.

BURP !

Max waited… and waited… and waited… but nothing happened.

Then he flushed the toilet. The red car vanished.
"Burp!" went the toilet.

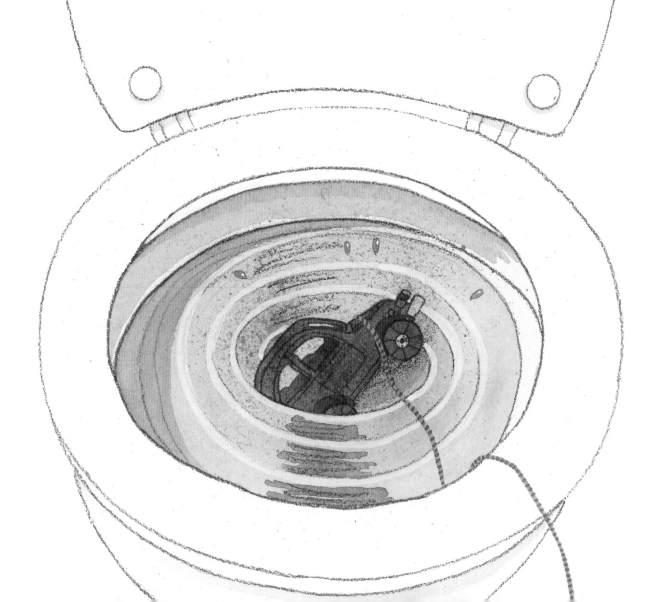

Max pulled the string out but there was nothing there. The monster had kept the little red car!

Max was sad and happy at the same time.

Max wasn't afraid of the toilet any more. He spent lots of time in the bathroom and he often flushed the toilet just to hear the gargling and the gurgling.

Max liked to bring his
toys in and leave them
out on the floor, just in
case the monster came
out to play.
Dad put up some shelves
for all the toys and
books.

Mum stuck up Max's best drawings on the
door so that everyone could see them when
they went to the toilet.

And she put up a new light so that Max could read his books and comics. Max loved to sit on the toilet and read for hours. It was so peaceful …

...though the toilet still gurgled and gargled
from time to time.